TITCHY WITCH

and the

Wobbly Fang

For Isobel Louise - welcome
R.I.

To Sarah and Sam
K.M.

ORCHARD BOOKS
338 Euston Road, London NW1 3BH
Orchard Books Australia
Hachette Children's Books
Level 17/207 Kent Street, Sydney, NSW 2000
First published in Great Britain in 2003
First paperback publication in 2004
ISBN 978 1 84121 050 6 (HB)
ISBN 978 1 84121 126 8 (PB)
Text © Rose Impey 2003 Illustrations © Katherine McEwen 2003
The rights of Rose Impey to be identified as the author and
Katherine McEwen to be identified as the illustrator of this work
have been asserted by them in accordance with the
Copyright, Designs and Patents Act, 1988.
A CIP catalogue record for this book is available from the British Library.
1 3 5 7 9 10 8 6 4 2 (HB)
5 7 9 10 8 6 4 (PB)
Printed in China
Orchard Books is a division of Hachette Children's Books, an Hachette Livre UK company.
www.hachettelivre.co.uk

TITCHY WITCH

and the

Wobbly Fang

Rose Impey ★ Katharine McEwen

ORCHARD BOOKS

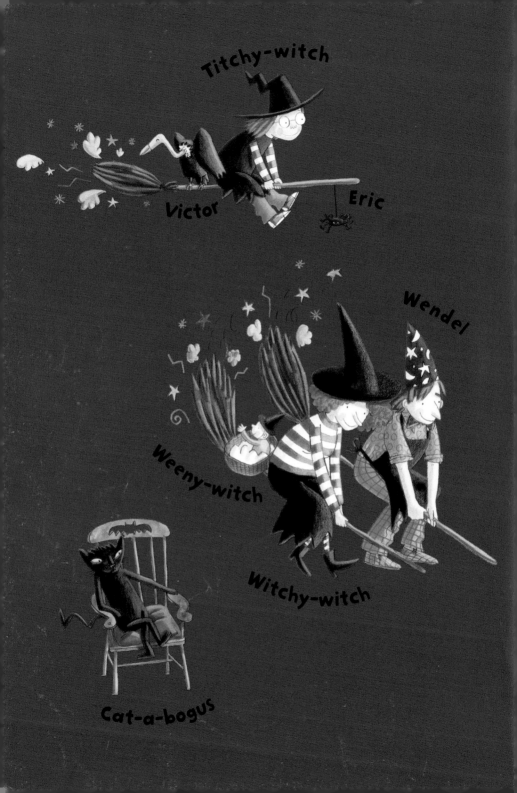

Titchy-witch

Victor

Eric

Wendel

Weeny-witch

Witchy-witch

Cat-a-bogus

Titchy-witch had a wobbly fang.
It wibble-wobbled all the time
and she didn't like it. "Yuk!"

"Leave it alone," said Cat-a-bogus. "It will come out when it's good and ready."

But Titchy-witch couldn't wait for that.

She and Dido tried to pull it out.

But the fang just wasn't ready.

Titchy-witch wanted a spell to make it fall out.
But Dad was busy in his workshop...

...and Mum said, "What would the Fang Fairy say?"

Titchy-witch didn't know about the Fang Fairy.

"When a fang comes out,"
Witchy-witch told her, "you put
it under your pillow. Then, if
you're good, the Fang Fairy
brings you a surprise."

Titchy-witch loved surprises.
She wanted hers this minute.

She decided to make a spell
of her own.
"Come on, Dido," she said.
"This should be easy-breezy."

As soon as Mum was out of the way, she borrowed a few magic ingredients.

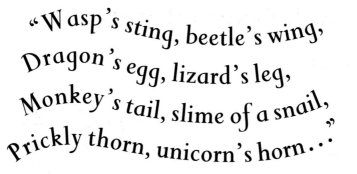

"Wasp's sting, beetle's wing,
Dragon's egg, lizard's leg,
Monkey's tail, slime of a snail,
Prickly thorn, unicorn's horn..."

Titchy-witch thought that should be enough.

Dido thought it might be too much!

Then she said some special magic
words: "Hocus pocus,
Bim Bala Bang
Please pull out…"

Titchy-witch was about to say,
"this wobbly fang."
But she had an even better idea.

Mum said the Fang Fairy would bring one surprise present for each of her fangs.
How many presents would she bring for all her fangs?

Titchy-witch started again:

"Hocus pocus,
Bim Bala Bang
Please pull out
all my fangs…"

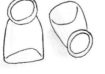

Clitter, clatter, clitter, clatter.
A whole set of little fangs fell out
and rolled round the kitchen floor.

Titchy-witch looked a bit funny
with no fangs.

Dido thought she looked
a bit scary.

But Titchy-witch wasn't too
worried...

...until Cat-a-bogus called her for tea.

It was hard eating termites on toast without any fangs.

Titchy-witch was keeping very quiet too. The cat soon knew something was wrong.

Cat-a-bogus was mad. In fact, he was furious.

He made Titchy-witch empty
her pockets.

Then the cat made some magic
of his own. Most of the fangs
went back.

All except one, which wibble-wobbled a bit.
Then it kept on falling out.

Next day, Titchy-witch found a
shiny silver slovrin under her
pillow. That would buy lots of
chocolate grobblies.

And she still had lots more fangs
to go.

TITCHY WITCH

Rose Impey ★ Katharine McEwen

Enjoy a little more magic with all the Titchy-witch tales:

All priced at £4.99 each

Colour Crunchies are available from all good
bookshops, or can be ordered direct from the publisher:
Orchard Books, PO BOX 29, Douglas IM99 1BQ
Credit card orders please telephone 01624 836000
or fax 01624 837033
or e-mail: bookshop@enterprise.net for details.

To order please quote title, author and ISBN
and your full name and address.
Cheques and postal orders should be
made payable to 'Bookpost plc'.
Postage and packing is FREE within the UK
(overseas customers should add £1.00 per book).

Prices and availability are subject to change.